King of the Kooties

King

of the

Kooties

Debbie Dadey

Illustrations by Kevin O'Malley

Walker & Company

New York

First published in the United States of America in 1999
by Walker Publishing Company, Inc.

Published simultaneously in Canada by Fitzhenry and Whiteside,
Markham, Ontario L3R 4T8

Library of Congress Cataloging-in-Publication Data
Dadey, Debbie.
King of the kooties/Debbie Dadey; illustrations by Kevin O'Malley
p. cm.
Summary: Nate's new friend Donald is being teased by the
meanest girl in fourth grade, but after several failed attempts,
he comes up with a plan to make her stop.
ISBN 0-8027-8709-6 (hardcover)
[1. Teasing Fiction. 2. Bullies Fiction. 3. Schools fiction.]
I. O'Malley, Kevin, 1961– ill. II. Title.
PZ7.D128Ki 1999
[Fic]—dc21   99-13054
CIP

BOOK DESIGN BY JENNIFER ANN DADDIO

Printed in the United States of America

2 4 6 8 10 9 7 5 3 1

To my wonderful family:

Eric, Nathan, Becky,

and Alex.

I love you all.

—D. D.

Contents

King of the Kooties

One

Doomsday

It had to happen. Today was the day. The first day of fourth grade, otherwise known as Doomsday. My name is Nate Nelson, and I don't mind telling you that school is not the favorite thing on my list. If I had a list of favorite things, that is, school would probably be the one-millionth thing.

Anyway, it had to happen. Summer was over. I was walking to school with my new neighbor, Donald. We both had on brand-new backpacks filled with fresh, unused notebooks and unsharpened pencils.

We had spent most of the summer doing my number-one favorite thing, playing baseball. I have to admit that Donald is almost as good at baseball as I am.

I had thought it would be a horrible summer. After all, my one and only good friend, Josh, had moved to Nebraska. Donald's family had moved into Josh's old house. At first I hated Donald for being in Josh's house when I wanted Josh there. Then Donald asked me to play baseball. I figured anyone who liked baseball couldn't be all bad. It ended up being one of the best summers I'd ever had, but I wouldn't have admitted it to my old friend Josh.

"All good things must come to an end," Donald said, like he was reading my mind.

"Why is that?" I wondered out loud. "Why can't we just play baseball every day for the rest of our lives?"

"School can be fun too," Donald said as we walked onto the playground.

I stopped short and looked at him like he was a monster from Mars. "Have you lost your mind?" I asked. "School isn't, and never will be, as fun as baseball."

"Well, that goes without saying," Donald agreed. I looked at Donald. Maybe he liked school better than me. I figured he was probably smarter than me, since he read a lot of books during the summer. Of course, anyone could be smarter than me in spelling. When we had spelling bees in third grade I always sat down first, even if the word was something simple like "piano."

Maybe Donald would be more popular than me. I guess you could say I'm a little shy. After all, I'd always hung around with Josh. Nobody else at school ever paid much attention to me. I'd never cared either. I didn't need anyone else as long as Josh had been around. Now, luckily, I had Donald as a friend. At least I hoped Donald would still like me after he met other kids at school. I was a little worried about it.

My sister Judy had walked ahead of us all the way to school. She was only in third grade and had never figured out that school was nothing to get excited about. She had actually looked forward to the first day of school and getting new school clothes. Now she was standing beside the bulletin board in the school yard that posted which teacher everyone had. About a million other kids were crowded around her.

"Nate!" she screamed when Donald and I walked onto the school sidewalk. "You and Donald both have Mrs. Gibson."

"All right," Donald and I said together. Maybe fourth grade would be okay with Donald in my classroom. I'd even heard that Mrs. Gibson was an okay teacher, as teachers go.

"Uh-oh. Louisa Albertson has her too," Judy yelled.

"Oh, no," I moaned, "not Louisa!"

Two

Dog Meat

"Who's Louisa?" Donald asked.

"Have you ever heard of a tornado?" I asked.

Donald nodded his head. "I was even in one once," he bragged.

"Well, take a tornado and wrap an earthquake and a flood up with it. Then you'll have something that's only half as terrible as Louisa," I said.

Donald laughed. "She can't be that bad."

"She's the worst thing that could happen to any school," I told Donald. "She likes to pick on people."

"We had a girl like that at my last school," Donald said, hanging his head.

"What did she do?" I asked.

Donald shrugged his shoulders and looked at his new school tennis shoes. I could tell he didn't want to answer, but I kept asking.

"You can tell me," I said. "What did this girl do?"

Donald sighed and spilled his guts. "She picked on me mostly. She always called me porcupine-head. She got the whole school calling me that, except for my friend Steve."

I felt embarrassed for Donald, so I quickly said, "That's just the way Louisa is. She lives to tease people. I think she must have been dropped on her head as a baby. It made her crazy."

"The best way to deal with jerks like that is to ignore them," Donald said. "Pretty soon, they get tired of teasing and leave you alone. It always worked at my old school."

"I don't know if that will work with Louisa," I said truthfully.

"Did she ever pick on you?" Donald asked.

I nodded sadly, remembering the time in first grade when she'd put mustard in my mittens. The teacher thought I had a terrible skin disease and sent me to the office. Louisa had laughed her head off over that one. "Yeah," I told Donald, "she's picked on me plenty of times."

Then over Donald's shoulder I saw something that put chills in my heart. Louisa was heading our way. I looked around, but there was nowhere to hide. I stood up straight, determined to take it like a man. It was only right to warn Donald.

"Donald," I said, putting my hand on his shoulder. "Be tough, she's right behind you."

"Hel-looo!" Louisa said with a big toothy smile. "Did they open the zoo today?"

"Very funny, Louisa," I said. "Go poison someone else with your charm." I don't care what Donald said. I wasn't about to let Louisa get away with giving me a hard time ever again.

That's when Donald made his fatal mistake.

He turned around and smiled at Louisa. Now, maybe I didn't mention it, but Donald is a little different. Everything is normal about him, except for one thing. His brown hair is very short and stands straight up like a crazy person's. When I first met him, I thought he was weird. Then I got to know him. He's really easy to talk to and likes to goof off just like Josh did.

But I could tell by the look on Louisa's face that she wasn't going to give Donald a chance. Donald was dog meat.

Three

Bad Hair

"Well, what have we here? Talk about a bad hair day," Louisa said with an evil grin. "The last time I saw hair like yours, I was at the circus."

"Leave Donald alone," I told Louisa.

But Louisa was just getting started. "There was a big monkey with pointy hair like yours at the circus. You even smell like that monkey." Louisa held her nose and giggled.

"Give us a break," I told Louisa. "It's the first day of school." I tried to be nice to Louisa, but it was hopeless. It was like standing in front of a speeding freight train and trying to stop it with a Ping-Pong ball. Her big green eyes were shining like a madman's and her hair reminded me of a science experiment gone bad.

"No, it wasn't the circus," Louisa said, tapping a finger against her pointy chin. "It was the warthog exhibit at the county fair! Donald, maybe you should enter. You'd win first prize!"

Donald just looked at Louisa. His face was red, but he didn't say a word. I was ready for him to blast her with a good comeback, but he did absolutely nothing. It was like he was in zombie-land. Surely he realized that Louisa was not the type to give up. She wouldn't quit teasing until Donald did something serious or moved away or died from old age.

"No," Louisa continued, "I think you can do better than warthog winner, you're more like a nerd or a kootie."

Donald didn't say a word. He just stared at his shoes and scratched his head.

"That's it!" Louisa jumped up and down, clapped her hands, and squealed. She acted like she had just cured the common cold. Amber and Emily, two of Louisa's friends, gathered around us and giggled. You'd think one of the girls would be a little nice, but not Louisa's friends. They were all rotten, just like Louisa.

I'd had all I could take. "Knock it off," I told her as I stepped in front of Donald.

"And miss all this fun?" Louisa smiled and pushed me aside. "I really have to talk with my friends, but first I must tell you my idea." By this time a lot of kids from the school yard had started gathering around us. I guess they were hoping for a fight. Louisa noticed they were watching, so she gave them a show.

Louisa adjusted her red book bag onto one shoulder and pulled out a brand-new pencil. She put her pencil on Donald's shoulder and looked at him seriously. "Donald," she said loud enough for everyone to hear. Her voice sounded like some old snotty queen from a faraway land. "From henceforth, you shall be known as Sir Donald, King of the Kooties!"

Amber and Emily clapped before patting Louisa on the back. Louisa giggled, wiped the

pencil on the grass, and then jabbed the pencil behind her right ear. "Now I'll leave you alone," she said, with a wave of her hand. "After all, I certainly wouldn't want to get your kooties!"

Donald just stood there with his mouth hanging open as Louisa bounced away, taking Amber and Emily with her. I don't usually think about violence, but just then I would have loved to bop Louisa right in the nose. A big, fat black-and-blue nose was exactly what she deserved, along with her disgusting friends.

"Come on, Donald," I said, nudging him on the shoulder as the rest of the crowd wandered away. "Don't let her bother you. That's just the way she is. Louisa is plain, stinking rotten. We'd better get to class."

Donald didn't move. His face wasn't red anymore, but the tips of his ears were bright crimson. For a minute I thought he was going to cry. Thankfully, he didn't. But he did ask a question.

"Are kooties bad?" he whispered.

Four

Kooties

"What planet did you grow up on?" I asked. "Everybody knows that kooties are terrible."

Donald had this really blank look on his face. My neighbor was obviously the only fourth-grader in the entire world who had never heard of kooties. "What exactly *are* kooties?" he asked.

"Kooties are—" I started to explain, but it wasn't as easy as I'd thought. "They're these little things."

"What kind of things?" Donald asked.

How could I explain kooties? They were unexplainable. "Didn't anyone ever have kooties at your old school?" I asked Donald.

Donald shook his head. "No, I've never heard of them."

Donald's old school must have been really weird. I shrugged and looked around for help. Most of the kids were standing by the bulletin board again. Some were already heading into the school building. I didn't see one kootie expert in the whole bunch. There was my sister Judy, but she didn't know much of anything. I figured it was up to me.

I took a deep breath and tried to explain one of the great mysteries of elementary school to my deprived neighbor. "Kooties," I began, "are these tiny creatures that invade kids that no one wants to be around."

"What do they look like?" Donald asked.

I shook my head. "No one knows," I said truthfully.

"Do they itch?" Donald asked.

I could tell Donald wasn't even close to catching on. I didn't understand how Donald

could be in fourth grade and not know about kooties. Even my little sister Judy knew about kooties. Of course, Judy probably had kooties. "No," I said. "They don't itch. They can't itch because they don't really exist. They're just made up."

Donald scratched the side of his head and looked at me like I was playing a video game with my toes. "If they don't exist, then how can I have them?" he asked.

Judy came up beside us and interrupted. "Guess what? I have Mrs. Gardner for a teacher."

"That's nice," I said just to get rid of her. I don't know why she'd think I'd care what teacher she had.

"She's brand-new and very pretty," Judy informed us. "Melody Branson told me so."

"That's nice," I repeated. "Would you get lost? I'm trying to explain something to Donald."

"What?" Judy asked in her perky little third-grade way.

"Nothing," I said quickly, but Donald blurted out, "Kooties," at the same time.

"E-ew!" Judy squealed. "Who has kooties?"

"Nobody, except you," I snapped. "Will you leave us alone?" I really didn't want to be seen with my silly little sister. Besides, the bell would probably ring any second, and I had to explain about kooties before it did.

"Can you tell me what kooties are?" Donald asked Judy.

Judy's eyes got big. "If you have kooties, no one wants to touch you or be around you."

"But what are they?" Donald insisted.

"I don't know." She giggled. "And I don't care, but I never want to see your underwear!"

"Just get lost," I told Judy. "Or I'll tell everyone you wear teddy-bear underwear."

Judy's face got a little red, and she walked off in a huff. She ran to catch up with a friend, then went inside the school building. I was running out of time, and I still didn't know what to tell Donald.

Donald may be a smart kid, maybe a little too

smart. There had to be a way to explain kooties so even he could understand. I would have to try a different approach. Unfortunately, I didn't get the chance.

Louisa's friends, Amber and Emily, gathered around us. I could tell from their monsterlike grins that this was not a social call. They were out for blood. Donald was their victim.

The girls giggled and then started chanting. "Circle, circle. Dot. Dot." They drew pretend circles on their arms and then poked the inside of the circles. "Now I've got my kootie shot," they sang.

> "Circle, circle. Dot. Dot.
> Now I've got my kootie shot."

I pulled Donald away. "Let me tell you, you may not be able to see kooties," I said, "but they are bad. Really bad."

"How do I get rid of them?" Donald asked.

"We need a plan," I said.

Five

Duck Soup

"Nate, what should I do?" Donald asked. I didn't answer him because the bell rang. It's a good thing it rang, because I wasn't sure what to tell him anyway.

Our school is about a hundred years old. It has these big stone steps that everybody has to squeeze on in order to get through the doorway. I wasn't really in a hurry to get to class, but there was no sense starting the year off in a bad way by being late. I showed Donald down the black-and-white tile hallway to the fourth-grade rooms.

Mrs. Gibson's room was number twelve. There were already about fifteen kids inside looking for a desk with their name on it. I knew some of the boys from playing Little League baseball and some of them from school last year. A few of them said hi to me. I didn't recognize any of the girls. Nobody said anything to Donald.

The room looked like every other classroom I'd ever been in, except for one thing. Along the back wall stood five brand-new computers. My other classrooms had always had just one old computer in the corner. Half the time they'd been broken, but these computer screens were alive with bright colors of what looked like neat games.

"Great," Donald said, "we had computers like this at my old school."

"Do you know how to play these games?" I asked.

"Sure," Donald told me. "I had more points than anyone in my old class."

I smiled. Donald could help me on these

computers, if I needed help. That is, if he didn't decide to hang around with someone else in Mrs. Gibson's class. I figured fourth grade might be okay.

I was wrong. For one little tiny moment I had forgotten about Louisa. Her screeching voice brought me back to reality. "Ewwwwww-weeeeee!" Louisa screamed when she came into the room. "I have to be in the same room with the Kootie King? This is horrible!"

I agreed. I would rather be hung upside down and tickled with an eagle feather than have to be in the same room with Louisa for one min-ute, let alone a whole year. Donald must have felt the same way, because his face was turning red again. The whole class looked around to see what Louisa was fussing about. A lot of the girls were giggling and pointing.

Thankfully, Mrs. Gibson looked too. "Louisa P. Albertson," Mrs. Gibson said very loudly. Everyone in the school knew Louisa because of her big, mean mouth. "Take a seat," Mrs. Gib-

son told Louisa, "and in the future you may keep your rude remarks to yourself."

Now it was Louisa's turn to have red cheeks. I smiled and took a seat on the opposite side of the room from Louisa. Donald sat beside me, and we both looked at Mrs. Gibson.

Our new teacher only stood a little taller than Louisa, but she didn't seem like the kind of teacher anyone could push around. She was pretty sturdy-looking and about as old as my mom. I felt a little sorry for her; after all, she probably felt as bad about having Louisa in class as we did.

Donald had to learn how to handle Louisa if he was going to make it through this year. So as kids continued to find seats I whispered to Donald, "Why didn't you say something to Louisa?"

Donald shrugged. "Why didn't you?" he asked in an innocent voice.

"She made fun of *you*," I told him. "You've got to stand up for yourself."

Donald looked at me and ran his fingers through his mess of hair. I didn't like the way he looked at me. It made me feel guilty. What was I supposed to do? Knock Louisa's head off for him?

Louisa's eyes were boring a hole in Donald and me. Things were getting worse and worse. Now Louisa probably held Donald personally responsible for Mrs. Gibson embarrassing her in front of the whole class. Donald was going to have to toughen up, or Louisa would flatten him like a load of bricks running over a cereal box.

"Welcome to fourth grade," Mrs. Gibson said, looking around the room. Every kid was in a seat and quiet. "I'm delighted that you are in my class. I know we will have a very good year together. I want this year to be a wonderful ex- perience for you."

Wonderful would be playing baseball. Com- pared to this, taking out the garbage would be wonderful. Right now, wonderful would be any- thing but sitting in the same room with Louisa. It felt like Donald and I were little ducks in a carnival, and Louisa had a big air gun aimed right at us. We were duck soup.

Six

Rotten Recess

Our playground is big. It's big enough for all of the third- and fourth-graders to play outside at the same time. There are exactly sixteen swings, three metal jungle gyms, and fifteen huge tires sticking up out of the ground for us to jump over. Best of all, our playground has two huge soccer fields to run in. With all that space, you would think that Donald could stay away from Louisa.

Not true. It was only the third day of school, and so far every day at recess Louisa had managed to find us and torment Donald. She had gotten quite a few other kids to join in with her. You'd think they'd have better things to do than bug us. Louisa and her friends left me with a pukey taste in my mouth that stayed the entire recess, even if Louisa just teased Donald for a few minutes. I didn't think I could take any more, especially since Donald wouldn't stand up for himself.

I was determined she wouldn't find us today, but we weren't outside for more than three minutes when we heard Louisa's screeching. "Look, there's the Kootie King!"

"Come on," I said, grabbing Donald's arm. "Let's play soccer."

"I don't know how," Donald told me. Sometimes I couldn't figure Donald out. How could he be so good at baseball and not even know how to play soccer?

"It's either soccer or Louisa," I yelled, running toward the soccer field and a gang of kids starting up a game. Donald must have seen Louisa coming, because he followed me.

Jason Samuels saw us coming. He had been in my third-grade class last year. "Hey, you guys can be on my team," he called.

"Thanks," I said, grateful to escape Louisa. I have to tell you that I'm pretty good at soccer and baseball. I like both, but I could tell Donald only liked baseball. Because frankly, he stunk at soccer. He didn't kick the ball once and fell down half the time. It didn't matter though, because when the bell rang we were safe. We had made it through the entire recess without having to listen to any more of Louisa's teasing.

I hadn't counted on the fact that Louisa is probably one of the most stubborn people in the world. If she is determined to tease someone, nothing will stop her. So Louisa pounced on us beside the door.

"Hey, Kootie Man," she yelled at Donald. "How's life in the Kingdom of Kooties?"

Donald turned red, and I turned mad. What gave Louisa the right to be so mean? I wanted to bop her right in her big rotten mouth. I wanted to turn her upside down and paint her face with Tabasco sauce, but I didn't do anything but fold my arms.

"Come on," Donald said, pulling me toward the building.

"Run away, Kootie Boy," Louisa told Donald. "If I had a face like yours, I'd shave my head and walk backward with a wig on my face." Amber and Emily gathered around us. Of course, they were laughing.

Something inside me exploded. "You'd better leave Donald alone," I shouted.

Louisa grew taller as I yelled. She towered over me and put her hands on her hips. "Why," she said, "who's going to stop me?"

I looked at Louisa. I don't fight much, although in kindergarten I did get into a fight with Billy Warren. He gave me a bloody nose and tore my good shirt right before school pictures were taken. I wasn't afraid to fight Louisa, but I could imagine the teasing I'd get if she beat me up. Besides, my mom told me to never hit a girl. As a matter of fact, my mom had told me never to fight anyone. But what was I supposed to do, let Louisa tear Donald to shreds with her words?

I put up my fists and faced Louisa.

Seven

Wimp

I am a wimp. I didn't fight Louisa. Of course, I might have fought her if Mrs. Gibson hadn't called us in from recess. If the truth were told, I'm just glad I didn't have to find out. Louisa is pretty big and mean. She must have drunk grow-juice as a baby, because she's at least a head taller than everyone in our class, except Mrs. Gibson. Louisa was barely a hair shorter than Mrs. Gibson. I'm just a normal not-too-tall fourth-grade boy named Nate with a Kootie King for a best friend. I haven't had a lot of experience fighting gorilla girls named Louisa.

I don't know how Mrs. Gibson did it. When she called us in for recess, she put her arm around Louisa. It was pretty disgusting. I've never seen a teacher even get close to Louisa. I know teachers have to be a little nice to their students, but they couldn't pay me enough to actually touch Louisa. That would be number one on my list of things I would never ever do. I don't have a list like that, but I'm sure that would be first if I did. Maybe that's why I didn't fight her. I would have had to touch her if I'd fought her.

"You know," I told Donald later as we walked home from school with Judy trailing along behind. "I would have fought Louisa for you."

Donald just looked at me without saying a word. I wasn't sure what he was thinking, but I didn't like the way he looked at me. He walked with his head hung low like a dog that'd just been yelled at for peeing on the carpet.

"Would you like to play some baseball?" I asked him as we walked into my yard. I figured if anything would cheer him up, baseball would.

"No, thanks," Donald said. "I'll guess I'll start on my homework." This was worse than I thought. Louisa was really getting to him.

"Look," I told Donald. "Don't worry about Louisa. I've been trying to think of a plan to deal with her."

Donald looked at me like he didn't know whether to believe me or not. "Thanks," he said, pointing to the ball lying in the grass, "but I was thinking maybe you could teach me how to play soccer. I can do my homework later."

I smiled. There was hope for Donald yet. I dropped my backpack in the yard and kicked my old black-and-green soccer ball toward him. Donald tried to kick it, he really did, but he ended up falling down on top of his backpack.

"That's okay," I told Donald, "I used to do that all the time. It just takes practice." I didn't tell him I was only five when I fell down like that, because I figured he felt bad enough as it was.

We played for at least an hour. I was sweating and so was Donald. I must be a pretty good teacher, because Donald started kicking the ball without falling down. He wasn't as good as me, but he wasn't bad.

"See," I told him. "All it took was a little practice, and you're practically an expert."

"Thanks," Donald told me. "I guess I'd better go home and work on my book report and math."

I rolled my eyes. Mrs. Gibson was an okay teacher—after all, she didn't let Louisa get the best of her. But I couldn't believe she'd already assigned a book report. "It should be against the law to have a book report due on the fourth day of school," I complained to Donald.

Donald shrugged. "It's not so bad. After all, we read the book in class."

"Book reports are the worst," I told Donald. "I'd rather have dried mud stuck up my nose than do a book report."

"I'm doing mine on my computer," Donald explained. "It prints in color. I can add neat pictures and borders."

I didn't say anything. I didn't have a com-puter, although I wanted one.

"Why don't you come over to my house?" he asked. "I'll show you how to do it. We'll have the best book reports in the whole class. Afterward, I'll show you my new computer game."

"Thanks," I told Donald. I kicked my soccer ball into the bushes, and we headed over to his house.

Donald's room is pretty cool. As a matter of fact, it's a kid's heaven. He has his own computer and color printer and his own TV. Donald showed me how to add pictures to my report. I had to admit it looked pretty good by the time we were finished.

I smiled at Donald. He might look a little different with his hair that sticks up all over, but hair doesn't matter that much. What matters is that he's a great guy to hang around with and he doesn't mind helping out a kid who doesn't have a computer. He could have kept his computer all to himself. I vowed right then and there that somehow, some way, I was going to stop Louisa from calling him the King of the Kooties.

Eight

Hit List

My dad travels a lot for his job, which is a real
pain. The only good part about it is that he
brings Judy and me lots of neat stuff from all
over the world. I have a backpack from Hong
Kong, a nutcracker from Germany, and T-shirts
from practically everywhere. When we have to
do a report on a country, I always have something to take for show and tell.

The bad thing about having a dad who travels
a lot is not being able to talk to him. My mom
is nice, but she doesn't understand about guy
stuff. If I told her about the trouble with Louisa,

Mom would probably tell me to ignore Louisa and she'd leave us alone. Let me tell you, we've already tried that, and it didn't work.

My sister, Judy, is no help either. She doesn't know what it's like to have a bully pick on her. She's this perfect little kid that no one would ever bother. She's so perfect and perky it's sickening. She hardly ever even gets in trouble at home, let alone at school.

My dad would understand, if he had been home. He was going to be in Puerto Rico for five more days, and by that time Louisa would have driven me crazy. He calls almost every night, but it's hard to talk about stuff like that on the phone, especially since my mom would be listening. I had to solve the problem with Louisa by myself.

That evening in my room, I got out a long yellow pad of paper and wrote in big fat letters at the top: LOUISA HIT LIST. Then I chewed on my eraser, trying to figure out how to keep her from teasing Donald. I couldn't think of anything. Nothing.

Then I remembered how Mrs. Gibson said to write with a wild mind to come up with ideas and write stories. So that's just what I did—I went wild. This is my list:

1. Tie Louisa to a tree and pour honey on her. Then drop an ant farm on her.

2. Sew her book bag shut with her homework inside.

3. Sprinkle hot pepper on her lunch and turn off all the water fountains.

4. Pour green paint on her hairbrush and take pictures when she gave herself green hair.

5. Put mud and ink in her notebook, pencil case, and backpack.

6. Announce over the intercom that Louisa sleeps with a night-light, teddy bear, and blankie.

7. Buy Louisa a one-way ticket to China.

8. Tell the president that Louisa is really a spy for the enemy.

9. Follow Louisa home and nail the door shut on her house.

10. Buy a really mean dog and teach it to eat Louisa.

When I finished number ten, Judy knocked on my bedroom door and walked inside. "Nate," she whined. "I have a problem."

"Go away," I told her. I didn't have time for messing around. I had to help Donald.

Judy looked at me with her big sad brown eyes and left the room. I felt a little guilty, but not enough to go after her. How bad could her problem be anyway? She probably lost a high heel to one of her dolls.

I got back to my yellow pad of paper. When I read the list out loud, I knew some of the things would work and some would get me in big trouble. I still wished I could talk to my dad. Then I remembered something my dad had told me. "Sometimes," he had said, "the best plan is to kill them with kindness."

That was it! I was going to kill Louisa with kindness.

Nine

Killing Her Softly

"Come on over," I told Donald on the phone. "I have a plan to stop Louisa dead in her tracks."

"Murder is illegal in most states," Donald said.

"Don't worry," I said. "The kind of killing I'm talking about is perfectly legal."

"All right," Donald said in a puzzled voice. "I'll be right over."

Five minutes later Donald and I were sitting on my bedroom floor. "What's your plan?" Donald asked.

"Louisa is the meanest person alive," I told Donald, like he didn't already know that for a fact.

Donald shrugged. "I guess so."

"My plan is to do the unexpected," I explained. "It's like in football. The way to win is to fake out the other team. Throw when they think you'll run."

Donald had this really blank look on his face. "I don't know how to play football," he said.

"It doesn't matter," I said. "We're going to kill her with kindness. Do nice things to her until we make her so sick she'll turn green. Basically, we're going to drive her crazier than she already is."

A big smile of recognition slowly crept over Donald's face. "Do you think it will work?"

"Louisa will never tease you again. She'll never even want to see your face, much less tease you." I felt like a hero. We were going to make this plan work. Donald would be free from Louisa, and so would I.

"Let's do it," Donald said.

I jumped up from the floor and grabbed my notebook. "Now you're talking. Here's Plan A." I showed Donald the page where I'd written "Sabotage with Sweetness."

"Are we going to poison her?" he asked.

"No, we're going to make cookies," I said triumphantly.

Donald didn't look too sure about the whole thing, but he followed me into the kitchen. Together we put the chocolate, sugar, peanut butter, and oatmeal for my mom's no-bake cookies in a big bowl. They're these really sweet, chewy chocolate cookies. My mom and Judy love them, so I figured Louisa would, too. Luckily my mom always keeps the ingredients around in case she gets a chocolate craving, which happens about once a week. The cookies look like little brown blobs, but they are good, and the best thing is that they're easy to make.

We were plopping the cookie dough into big

lumps on a tray when Judy came into the kitchen. "Can I help?" she asked.

"No," I told her. "We're almost finished."

"Mom's going to be mad at the mess you made," Judy said in her typical little sister way.

"We'll clean it up," Donald said. He grabbed a sponge and started wiping up the peanut butter and chocolate. It made a big brown smear all over the kitchen counter.

"Will you help me with my problem now?" Judy asked.

"Can't you see we're busy?" I said.

Donald was nicer than me. Of course, he didn't have a little sister to irritate him. He continued smearing peanut butter all over the counter and tried to help Judy. "What's wrong?" he asked her.

Judy was silent for a minute. Then she blurted out, "My teacher hates me!" I have to admit she shocked me. Little Miss Perfect's teacher hated her? How could that be? After all, Judy never did anything wrong.

I stopped plopping cookies onto the tray and looked at Judy. Her lip quivered like she could cry at any second. She wasn't kidding.

"Why do you think your teacher hates you?" Donald said, rinsing out the sponge.

"She never calls on me," Judy explained. "She ignores me."

"Do you raise your hand?" Donald asked.

Judy nodded and stuck her finger in the cookie dough bowl. "I always raise my hand, even when she's not asking a question," she said, licking the dough off her finger.

"Maybe," Donald said slowly, "maybe you raise your hand too much."

I got it. Judy was driving her teacher crazy. Her teacher couldn't stand Judy because she was too perfect.

"But I know the answers," Judy said.

Donald nodded. "I know. But here's what I want you to do. We'll call it Operation Judy."

Judy's eyes were wide as Donald continued.

"Tomorrow don't raise your hand or even talk to your teacher unless she talks to you first."

Judy nodded. "Can I take her some cookies?"

Donald looked at me, and I shrugged. "Sure," Donald said, "but just give them to her. Don't talk."

Judy smiled at Donald and gave him a big hug. "Thank you. You're terrific."

I guess Judy didn't know about Donald being the Kootie King, or she never would have hugged him.

Ten

Stunk

To put it mildly, Plan A stunk. The next day before school Louisa took one look at our cookies and screeched. "Ew—whee! Those look like dog poop!"

Of course, Amber and Emily squealed like little pigs and started chanting. "Kootie Poop! Kootie Poop!" The school yard was pretty full of kids, and they all looked at me and Donald.

Poor Donald turned redder than I've ever seen him. When Louisa, Amber, and Emily walked away, he looked at me like a disaster victim. "That was definitely not a good idea," he said.

"That's okay, I'm ready with Plan B," I told him.

Donald didn't look excited about Plan B. "Maybe we should just keep ignoring Louisa. She'll eventually get tired of humiliating me."

I shook my head. "No, you don't know Louisa. We have to proceed with Plan B."

Donald sighed, "All right," he said, "what's next?"

"I'm glad you asked," I said, "because Plan B is Crumble with Compliments."

"That sounds like a dessert," Donald said.

"Just watch the master at work," I told him. I took a deep breath and walked up to Louisa. It made me a little ill to do what I had to do. I just hoped Donald appreciated what I was doing for him. "Louisa," I said in my sweetest voice, "you sure look pretty today."

Louisa's mouth dropped open, and every one of her huge teeth hung out. I didn't stop there

though, I kept going, trying not to sound smart-alecky. "Louisa, your hair is so beautiful. I bet you'll be a movie star when you grow up."

Louisa kept staring at me. I could feel my face turning dark red, but I didn't give up. My plan looked like it was working.

"Louisa," I said, hoping Donald would get the idea and come help me kill Louisa with kindness, because it was very hard to think of nice things to say about Louisa. "You must be the smartest girl in this entire school. It must be great to be so smart."

I'm not sure what I said, but Louisa didn't like it. She grabbed my shirt, and she didn't let go. I had the feeling that Plan B really stunk.

Eleven

Gorilla Warfare

"We've got to give up," Donald said as the last bell rang at the end of the day. "You were lucky Louisa didn't kill you this morning. If Mrs. Gibson hadn't come along, you would have been chopped liver." Everyone, including Donald and me, grabbed their book bags and hustled out of the classroom, except Louisa and Mrs. Gibson.

"We won't give up until we've won," I told Donald.

"Then we'll have to think of a new plan," Donald suggested. "A plan that doesn't involve chocolate or compliments."

I nodded. "With the right plan, Louisa will never bother us again." I couldn't help wondering what kind of trouble Louisa was in, since she was staying after school. I figured she probably picked on some other kids and Mrs. Gibson saw the whole thing. Now maybe Louisa would spend the rest of her life staying after school. Good. She deserved it.

Out of the corner of my eye I saw Louisa taking her math book up to Mrs. Gibson's desk. That seemed a little strange, but of course everything about Louisa was strange. The hard thing was figuring out how to deal with her.

I thought about it all during supper. I thought about it when Judy came in my room to complain about how her teacher hated her. "Why do you care?" I asked her. "What difference does it make if she hates you?"

Judy stared at me and shook her head. "It matters a lot to me," she said and slowly walked toward the door. I had to admit I hated seeing her depressed, I kind of missed the old bouncy Judy.

"Didn't Donald's plan work?" I asked Judy.

She shook her head, no. Her lip trembled as she said, "Mrs. Gardner didn't even call on me once. She hates me." Judy threw herself on my bed like a berserk actress and started crying.

I didn't know what else to do, so I patted her head. "You just need to keep trying," I told Judy. "I bet tomorrow if you don't raise your hand, Mrs. Gardner will call on you."

Judy looked up at me. Her nose was all runny, and she had probably gotten snot all over my bedspread. "Do you really think so?" she asked.

I nodded. "I'm sure."

Judy smiled and wiped her nose with the back of her hand. "I think I'll go paint Mrs. Gardner a picture. I'll give it to her, but I won't say a word."

"Good idea," I said, trying to sound encouraging even though I had no idea if Donald's plan would really work.

As Judy left, a lightbulb went off in my head. Judy had helped me with the perfect idea. I ran into the kitchen to call Donald.

"Just get over to my house and bring paint." I hung up the phone and got ready. I swiped three old T-shirts out of the rag bag in the laundry room. I couldn't find any used newspaper, so I snatched the paper off the porch. I hoped my mom wouldn't mind missing the evening news for just one day. I was grabbing some little paintbrushes from the garage when Donald came over. He was lugging two huge cans, one in each of his hands.

"What's that?" I asked him. "Are you moving to China?"

Donald put the cans down and looked at me. "You asked me to bring over paint, so I did."

"I meant little bitty containers of paint, like finger paint," I explained. "We don't need to paint a skyscraper."

"How was I supposed to know?" Donald asked. "These things weigh a ton, you'd better use them."

"Okay," I said, grabbing one heavy can. "Let's take them in my room, and I'll explain my plan."

Donald sat on the edge of my bed while I outlined my idea. It was simple: Keep being nice

to Louisa. We were going to be so nice we'd make her sick. As a matter of fact, I hoped she puked.

We had to beat her at her own game. Donald spread the newspapers out on the floor and put the T-shirts on top. I used a screwdriver to pry open one of the cans of paint. It was bright orange. "This is perfect," I told Donald. With a thin paintbrush I started making a big letter K on one of the shirts.

"Come on," I said, "start painting. I can't wait to see the look on Louisa's face."

"We can't be too mean," Donald said. "After all, my mom told me not to be mean to girls."

"Girl!" I shouted. "Louisa is a gorilla. She has embarrassed you since the beginning of school, and if you let her, she'll keep it up the whole year. Do you really want to go through the entire year with her teasing?"

Donald shook his head. "All right," he said, "give me a paintbrush."

"That's the spirit," I said. "It's time for some gorilla warfare."

Twelve

Mess

I knew those big cans of paint were a bad idea when I saw Donald carrying them. I was right.

I have green carpet in my room, which is fine because I have green walls. My mom put up a baseball border with green in it around the middle of the room. She even painted little green-and-white baseballs on the ceiling around my ceiling fan and in the corners. It's not a bad bedroom. That is, it wasn't until I spilled bright orange paint all over my green carpet.

The T-shirts were almost finished. They looked pretty darn good. I leaned back and held one up to check the writing. I knocked right into a paint can, and *blam*, the orange paint tumbled over. It flashed before my eyes like a horror movie. Bright orange paint went everywhere!

Donald pulled his shirt off and started dabbing up the paint. I did the same thing, but it was hopeless. It was practically an ocean of paint.

Donald used his hands to scoop big globs back into the bucket. I grabbed some papers off my desk and used it to funnel more paint back into the can. It took a while, but eventually we had most of the mess cleaned up. I looked at Donald. He was naked from the waist up. His arms were orange all the way to his elbows, and he even had orange paint splattered on his face and hair. He looked like a circus clown who'd been swimming in orange sauce. Either that, or a duck with a really bad hair day.

I guess I looked just as bad, because Donald glanced at me and cracked up. "You look

awful," he said. He fell on his back and rolled around laughing.

"Don't get any more paint anywhere," I warned him. "I'm in enough trouble as it is. My mom is going to kill me when she sees I've ruined my carpet."

Donald stopped laughing. "Listen," he told me. "We have a rug cleaner at my house. I know how to use it. Maybe it'll take up this stain."

Donald was all right. Maybe I'd live to see fifth grade after all, but maybe not. "We can't just lug a rug cleaner through the house," I said. "My mom will want to know what it's for."

"We'll sneak it in through the window," Donald told me.

I nodded. It just might work. I looked down at the papers I'd used to scoop paint. It was my book report, the same book report that was due tomorrow.

"This is just great," I complained to Donald. "I've ruined my room and my book report. My mom and Mrs. Gibson can take turns killing me."

Donald put his orange hand on my shoulder. "Don't worry. We'll clean your carpet, and I saved your book report on my computer. All we have to do is print it out again."

"Are you sure?" I asked him.

"Put yourself in my hands," he said. It's hard to trust someone who has orange hands, but I was desperate.

Thirteen

Secret Weapon

Carpet cleaners may not look heavy, but let me tell you, they are. They are especially heavy when you try to pull one up to a second-story window with bedsheets. I thought I was going to blow a gasket hauling it up, even though Donald helped me.

Donald stood below my window and tied my green bedsheets onto the carpet cleaner's handle. He grunted and lifted it up as high as he could. That was my signal to start pulling. I tugged my green sheets until my face turned purple, but the cleaner barely moved. It swayed a little bit, dangerously close to the living room window. "Watch out for the window," I hollered to Donald, but he was way ahead of me. He positioned himself between the window and the cleaner. If anything went through the window, it would be Donald.

"Okay," Donald said, "on the count of three, give it all you got."

I didn't have the heart to tell Donald I was giving it all I had, especially since his face was as red as a raspberry. "One," Donald said, "two, three."

I pulled with every ounce of strength I had, and Donald lifted. My hands burned from the effort. The carpet cleaner went up a little, then a little more. Finally it hung above Donald's head. "We're making it," I yelled, but I yelled too soon. The sheet started slipping out of my hands.

"Look out," I yelled to Donald. I could just picture Donald smashed on the ground underneath the cleaner. The paper would read: Cause

of death—zonked on the head with a carpet cleaner.

I didn't count on reinforcements. I didn't count on Judy. She came to the rescue like the cavalry. "Pull," she yelled in my ear. Together, we pulled the cleaner away from Donald.

In three seconds, Donald was behind Judy. The three of us pulled until the blue carpet cleaner handle appeared in my window. We all hauled it into my room.

"Thanks for helping," Donald told Judy.

"What in the world are you doing?" Judy asked us.

I shrugged, hoping Judy wouldn't notice my carpet. "I just thought I'd do a little cleaning."

"You never clean your room unless Mom makes you," Judy said. Then her eyes rested on the bright orange spot on my carpet.

"Oh, my gosh," Judy said. "Mom is going to kill you."

"Not if we get the stain out first," I told Judy.

Donald handed me a plastic container. "Fill this with water," he commanded. He pulled a plastic cleaning-fluid bottle out of his hip pocket and poured it into the machine while I went for water.

Judy sat on my bed and watched. I turned the sound up really loud on my clock radio, and Donald flipped on the switch to the cleaner. The music hid the noise of the carpet cleaner a little bit. Donald, Judy, and I took turns running the cleaner over the spot. Thankfully, Mom was down in the basement doing laundry, so she didn't come up to investigate. I have to admit most of the stain on my carpet did come up. The bright orange was gone. Now it was mostly a muddy brown. Donald, Judy, and I stared at the stain for a long time.

"Let's try the carpet cleaner again," Donald suggested. "Maybe it'll all come up."

"We'd better wait until tomorrow," I said. "I still have to redo my report."

Unfortunately, I didn't get the chance to do my report. My mom came in my room. "Nate," she said, "have you seen the newspaper?" She took one look at my rug and forgot all about current events. I thought she was going to have a heart attack.

"What's that on your carpet?" she screeched.

I gulped. "It's just a little paint."

"What were you painting in your room?" she asked, holding onto the wall for support.

Judy jumped up from her seat on my bed. "He was helping me with a school project."

Donald and I looked at Judy. I couldn't believe perfect little Judy was lying to save my skin.

"We'll clean it again," Donald told my mom.

My mom shook her head. "No, I'd better call the carpet company to see what they recommend." Mom looked at me before leaving the room. "You are grounded, mister. You should know better."

I fell back on my bed. "Great, now I can't even get my book report done."

"Don't worry," Donald told me. "I'll print another copy out for you."

Donald was true to his word. The next day I

had my newly printed report ready to turn in. We both had faded orange paint all over our hands, but we also had a secret weapon under our shirts. I had a smile on my face, in spite of all the trouble I was in. I almost wanted Louisa to tease us. I was disappointed we were late for school. We'd have to wait for recess to try our plan.

In the classroom Louisa never said a word to me or Donald. She stayed on her side of the room, which was fine with me. Mrs. Gibson stayed by Louisa's desk a lot, too. I figured Mrs. Gibson wanted to keep Louisa from misbehaving. I guess I could have figured wrong.

"Louisa," Mrs. Gibson was telling her when I went to sharpen my pencil, "the more you practice, the better you'll get."

"I can't do it," Louisa whined.

"You can," Mrs. Gibson told her firmly, "and I'll help you. The computers will help you practice, too."

I looked at Louisa and wondered what she

was having trouble with. We hadn't done any-thing too hard in fourth grade yet. Everything was still mostly review stuff from last year.

It was a mistake looking at Louisa. She saw me and gave me a look that would melt bricks. I gulped and sharpened my pencil. I figured Louisa would be ready to murder both Donald and me at recess. I patted my shirt. Louisa didn't know that we were ready for her this time. Just let her try to bother us. I was looking forward to recess.

Fourteen

Orange Boogers

I didn't have to wait long. The second Donald and I walked onto the playground, Louisa was on us like a dog on a ham bone. "Kootie King," she said in her disgusting high-pitched voice. "You're turning orange. Ew-ewwww! I never knew kooties were orange. Yuck!"

"That's right, Louisa," I said in a calm voice. "Kooties are orange, and we're like King Midas. Whoever we touch turns orange. First their hands turn orange. Then their face. Before long, their hair and their whole body is orange."

"That's disgusting," Louisa said. "I bet your

boogers are even orange." A few kids standing beside Louisa giggled.

Jason Samuels dropped his soccer ball and frowned at Louisa. "Why do you keep picking on him?" he asked. "What did he ever do to you?"

"Nothing," Louisa said, "and I plan to keep it that way. I don't want orange boogers, too."

Donald's face turned red instead of orange, but I was like James Bond. I was cool and deadly. "It's true," I told Louisa. "We have orange boogers. Everything is orange. Even our clothes are turning orange." I nodded to Donald, and at the same moment we pulled up our shirts.

All the girls gasped when they saw our T-shirts. Louisa just looked at us like we were crazy.

Louisa screamed out the words on our T-shirts. "King of the Kooties," she read off Donald's. "Friend of the King of the Kooties," she read off mine.

"We *are* the Kingdom of Kooties," Donald

said, just like we had rehearsed before school. "But we want our kingdom to grow."

"And grow it shall," I said with a laugh. "*You* will be the next member of the Kingdom of Kooties."

Donald whipped the third T-shirt out of his book bag. Several of the girls standing around Louisa read it out loud. "Louisa, Princess of Kooties."

"When pigs fly," Louisa said, not even one bit worried.

"Kooties are contagious," I said. "And we are going to share our kooties with you." I reached my hand toward Louisa. I felt like Count Dracula capturing my next victim. "We want you to be one of us," I told Louisa.

She shrieked and pulled away. "Touch me and I'll clobber you," she yelled.

"Don't get upset," I told Louisa. "We're your friends. We just want to share our kooties with you."

Donald smiled. "We're nice guys. What's ours is yours."

"You're disgusting," Louisa snapped.

"Why, Louisa," I said in the sweetest voice I could muster, "here we are trying to be nice, and you insult us. You hurt us to the core."

Donald made me proud. He held the shirt toward Louisa, and in a voice that sounded evil, he said, "It may not be today. It may not be tomorrow. But unless you stop teasing us, we will give you kooties, and you will be the Princess of Kooties."

Several of Louisa's friends giggled, and Louisa's face turned milk white. Jason Samuels laughed and said, "Way to go, guys!" Jason and a group of boys started chanting, "Kootie Princess. Kootie Princess!" They got louder and louder. Then they started jumping up and down and pounding their hands with their fists. Donald and I joined in. Kids from all over the playground came over to see what was happening. We just kept chanting, "Kootie Princess. Kootie Princess!"

"You guys are jerks," Louisa screamed. "I

never want to talk to you again!" She turned and stomped away.

I couldn't resist yelling after her, "We'll save your T-shirt in case you forget!" Donald waved the T-shirt at her, just to prove the point.

We had won! Judging from the look on Louisa's face, she wouldn't even look crossways at us ever again. Donald and I jumped up and down.

"Nate," Donald yelled and slapped me on the back. "You did it!"

"We both did it," I said.

"You really did do it!" Judy came running up to Donald and me. "You were right about Mrs. Gardner. She called on me today!"

Donald patted Judy on the back. "See, she does like you."

"She even smiled at me." Judy practically beamed, she was so happy. I was glad it had worked out for her, but I had to admit I was thrilled for Donald.

Fifteen

Smart Guy

"Dad!" I yelled. It was a few days after the kootie princess incident, and my dad was finally home. Mom and Judy kissed Dad and talked to him, then I finally got him all to myself.

"So how's fourth grade?" Dad asked.

I grinned. "My teacher's okay, but Louisa's in my class."

Dad sat down on the couch and put his hand on his forehead. "Not the same Louisa who put mustard in your mittens?" he asked.

"The very same one," I said, "but she won't

be picking on me or Donald anymore, and it's all because of you."

"Me?" Dad asked. "I wasn't even in the same state."

I sat down on the couch beside Dad. "It was your advice that helped," I told him. "Remember how you said that sometimes you have to kill with kindness?"

Dad nodded slowly as I pulled out the kootie shirts. I told Dad the whole awful story about how Louisa had teased Donald. "We used these shirts to get her. We offered to make her a member of the Kingdom of Kooties. Then the guys on the playground got on our side and started chanting, 'Kootie Princess. Kootie Princess!' I'm pretty sure Louisa won't be bothering us again."

Dad looked at the shirts, then looked at me. I didn't know for sure what he'd say. Would he be mad? Not my dad.

"I guess you did what you had to do," he said. He smiled and patted me on the back. I

wouldn't admit it to anyone at school, but my dad gave me a big hug.

I smiled and hugged back. I knew that if anyone could talk my mom out of being mad about the paint on my rug, it would be my dad. I was glad he was home.

The plan really did work. Louisa never teased Donald again, at least about kooties. I almost fainted one day when Louisa asked Donald to help her with a computer game. I watched them both in the back of the classroom. Louisa sat close to Donald, right in front of a computer. I even saw Louisa's arm brush against Donald's. She didn't notice, but I did. Louisa had turned out to be the Princess of Kooties after all.